D1429349

THE TALE OF
Ginger and Pickles

THE TALE OF
GINGER AND PICKLES

BY

BEATRIX POTTER

A PETER RABBIT™

110th Anniversary Edition

FREDERICK WARNE

DEDICATED WITH VERY KIND REGARDS TO OLD
MR. JOHN TAYLOR,
WHO "THINKS HE MIGHT PASS AS A DORMOUSE!"
(THREE YEARS IN BED AND NEVER A GRUMBLE!)

FREDERICK WARNE

Published by the Penguin Group
Penguin Books Ltd., 80 Strand, London WC2R 0RL, England
Penguin Group (USA) Inc., 375 Hudson Street, New York, New York 10014, USA
Penguin Group (Australia), 250 Camberwell Road, Camberwell,
Victoria 3124, Australia (a division of Pearson Australia Group Pty. Ltd.)
Penguin Group (Canada), 90 Eglinton Avenue East, Suite 700, Toronto,
Ontario M4P 2Y3, Canada (a division of Pearson Penguin Canada Inc.)
Penguin Books India Pvt. Ltd., 11 Community Centre, Panchsheel Park, New Delhi—110 017, India
Penguin Group (NZ), 67 Apollo Drive, Rosedale, Auckland 0632,
New Zealand (a division of Pearson New Zealand Ltd.)
Penguin Books (South Africa) (Pty.) Ltd, 24 Sturdee Avenue, Rosebank, Johannesburg 2196, South Africa

Penguin Books Ltd., Registered Offices: 80 Strand, London WC2R 0RL, England

Website: www.peterrabbit.com

First published by Frederick Warne in 1909
First published with reset text and new reproductions
of Beatrix Potter's illustrations in 2002
This edition published in 2011

003 - 10 9 8 7 6 5 4 3

Colour reproduction by
EAE Creative Colour Ltd, Norwich
Printed and bound in China

PUBLISHER'S NOTE

Originally entitled *Ginger and Pickles*, this was the second of Beatrix Potter's books to be published by Frederick Warne & Co. in a slightly larger format (177 mm x 138 mm), in order to show off her detailed illustrations. The manuscript was written in an exercise book and sent to Harold Warne in December 1908, partly for his approval and partly as a Christmas present for his daughter, Louie.

The storyline was slightly altered from Beatrix's original conception, as she wanted to include a character representing her local shopkeeper, John Taylor, who was now bedridden. He suggested he might pass as a dormouse, and so John Dormouse appears in the tale.

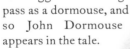

ONCE UPON A TIME there was a village shop. The name over the window was "Ginger and Pickles".

It was a little small shop just the right size for Dolls — Lucinda and Jane Doll-cook always bought their groceries at Ginger and Pickles.

The counter inside was a convenient height for rabbits. Ginger and Pickles sold red spotty pocket-handkerchiefs at a penny three farthings.

They also sold sugar, and snuff and goloshes.

In fact, although it was such a small shop it sold nearly everything—except a few things that you want in a hurry—like bootlaces, hair-pins and mutton chops.

Ginger and Pickles were the people who kept the shop. Ginger was a yellow tom-cat, and Pickles was a terrier.

The rabbits were always a little bit afraid of Pickles.

The shop was also patronized by mice — only the mice were rather afraid of Ginger.

Ginger usually requested Pickles to serve them, because he said it made his mouth water.

"I cannot bear," said he, "to see them going out at the door carrying their little parcels."

"I have the same feeling about rats," replied Pickles, "but it would never do to eat our customers; they would leave us and go to Tabitha Twitchit's."

"On the contrary, they would go nowhere," replied Ginger gloomily.

(Tabitha Twitchit kept the only other shop in the village. She did not give credit.)

Ginger and Pickles gave unlimited credit.

Now the meaning of "credit" is this — when a customer buys a bar of soap, instead of the customer pulling out a purse and paying for it — she says she will pay another time.

And Pickles makes a low bow and says, "With pleasure, madam," and it is written down in a book.

The customers come again and again, and buy quantities, in spite of being afraid of Ginger and Pickles.

But there is no money in what is called the "till".

The customers came in crowds every day and bought quantities, especially the toffee customers. But there was always no money; they never paid for as much as a pennyworth of peppermints.

But the sales were enormous, ten times as large as Tabitha Twitchit's.

As there was always no money, Ginger and Pickles were obliged to eat their own goods.

Pickles ate biscuits and Ginger ate a dried haddock.

They ate them by candle-light after the shop was closed.

When it came to Jan. 1st there was still no money, and Pickles was unable to buy a dog licence.

"It is very unpleasant, I am afraid of the police," said Pickles.

"It is your own fault for being a terrier; *I* do not require a licence, and neither does Kep, the collie dog."

"It is very uncomfortable, I am afraid I shall be summoned. I have tried in vain to get a licence upon credit at the Post Office," said Pickles. "The place is full of policemen. I met one as I was coming home.

"Let us send in the bill again to Samuel Whiskers, Ginger, he owes 22/9 for bacon."

"I do not believe that he intends to pay at all," replied Ginger.

"And I feel sure that Anna Maria pockets things — Where are all the cream crackers?"

"You have eaten them yourself," replied Ginger.

Ginger and Pickles retired into the back parlour.

They did accounts. They added up sums and sums, and sums.

"Samuel Whiskers has run up a bill as long as his tail; he has had an ounce and three-quarters of snuff since October.

"What is seven pounds of butter at 1/3, and a stick of sealing wax and four matches?"

"Send in all the bills again to everybody 'with compts'," replied Ginger.

After a time they heard a noise in the shop, as if something had been pushed in at the door. They came out of the back parlour. There was an envelope lying on the counter, and a policeman writing in a notebook!

Pickles nearly had a fit, he barked and he barked and made little rushes.

"Bite him, Pickles! bite him!" spluttered Ginger behind a sugar-barrel, "he's only a German doll!"

The policeman went on writing in his notebook; twice he put his pencil in his mouth, and once he dipped it in the treacle.

Pickles barked till he was hoarse. But still the policeman took no notice. He had bead eyes, and his helmet was sewed on with stitches.

At length on his last little rush
— Pickles found that the shop
was empty. The policeman had
disappeared.

But the envelope remained.

"Do you think that he has gone to fetch a real live policeman? I am afraid it is a summons," said Pickles.

"No," replied Ginger, who had opened the envelope, "it is the rates and taxes, £3 19 11¾."

"This is the last straw," said Pickles, "let us close the shop."

They put up the shutters, and left. But they have not removed from the neighbourhood. In fact some people wish they had gone further.

Ginger is living in the warren. I do not know what occupation he pursues; he looks stout and comfortable.

Pickles is at present a gamekeeper.

The closing of the shop caused great inconvenience. Tabitha Twitchit immediately raised the price of everything a half-penny; and she continued to refuse to give credit.

Of course there are the tradesmen's carts — the butcher, the fishman and Timothy Baker.

But a person cannot live on "seed wigs" and sponge-cake and butter-buns — not even when the sponge-cake is as good as Timothy's!

After a time Mr. John Dormouse and his daughter began to sell peppermints and candles.

But they did not keep "self-fitting sixes"; and it takes five mice to carry one seven-inch candle.

Besides — the candles which they
sell behave very strangely in warm
weather.

And Miss Dormouse refused to take back the ends when they were brought back to her with complaints.

And when Mr. John Dormouse was complained to, he stayed in bed, and would say nothing but "very snug"; which is not the way to carry on a retail business.

So everybody was pleased when Sally Henny-penny sent out a printed poster to say that she was going to re-open the shop — "Henny's Opening Sale! Grand co-operative Jumble! Penny's penny prices! Come buy, come try, come buy!"

The poster really was most 'ticing.

There was a rush upon the opening day. The shop was crammed with customers, and there were crowds of mice upon the biscuit canisters.

Sally Henny-penny gets rather flustered when she tries to count out change, and she insists on being paid cash; but she is quite harmless.

And she has laid in a remarkable assortment of bargains.

There is something to please everybody.

THE END